James and His Big Catch

Written By: Virginia C. Delos Reyes

Illustrated By: Anhelina Stepanova

Dedicated to my husband and son who are the inspirations behind this story. I love you!

1 Corinthians 13:13

In the early morning sunrise,
a tiny boat floats still on a lake.
James and his dad are on a fishing trip,
hoping to make a big catch on their date.

There are so many kinds of fish in the water
like seabass, bluegills, catfish, and more.
"Cast your fishing line James!"
"And be careful to not go overboard!"

The line sinks in.
James and his dad sit back to wait.
Time flies by with no movement in sight,
as fish keeps dodging and toying the bait.

James takes a look over the boat.
He spots some lily pads and a bull frog too!
But there is no fish to be seen,
so he made a frown and bid the frog adieu.

His dad smiles,
"My son, my son, be patient and still."
"I know waiting is hard,
but it's part of the thrill!"

Suddenly, the fishing rod made a twitch.
James jumps up to reel in his catch.
What can it be, what can it be- but some seaweed
and an old fisherman's hat?

His dad with a smirk gives him a pat.
"My son, my son, do not fret."
"You didn't make a catch this time,
just try again and you'll get a bite I bet."

With a loud groan and a "humph" too,
James casts his line a little farther.
He waits while watching his bobber dance.
Maybe this time there will be fish to catch underwater.

James felt a tug on his fishing rod.
He quickly made a pull.
What a tease, what a tease-
It's just a sock made out of wool!

"Daddy, can we go home now?"
"This trip is really no fun."
"I'm not good at fishing."
"I am angry and feeling tired under this hot sun."

"The third time is a charm my son, this I've heard."
"Have confidence, relax, and don't overreact."
"Patience is a virtue,
that is a true fact."

James puffs up his chest
and casts his line once more.
"Stay calm and be patient,
I'll catch this fish I'm sure."

The rod begins shaking rapidly.
James knew just what to do.
He counts, "one-two-three!"
And makes one big pull!

PLOP! That did the trick!
James drew something onto the boat's surface floor.
He can't believe his eyes,
and stares at it like it was a giant DINOSAUR!

His eyes big and wide open.
He giggles and gives a loud shout!
James so pleased with himself, he squeals,
"Look dad, I caught a big RAINBOW TROUT!"

The fish is so big and colorful.
It's orange, red, green, yellow, and blue.
James feels so happy.
He caught a fish of every color and every hue.

His dad gives him a big hug.
"You see my son, patience is the key."
"I am so proud of you today,
you truly are my patient boy indeed."

"But if we look forward to something we don't yet have,
we must wait patiently and confidently"

- Romans 8:25

The End

Made in the USA
Coppell, TX
12 October 2020